Bowwow Powwow

Bagosenjige-niimi'idim

www.mnhspress.org

The Minnesota Historical Society Press is a member of the Association of University Presses.

Manufactured in Canada

10 9 8 7 6 5 4 3 2

♾ The paper used in this publication meets the minimum requirements of the American National Standard for Information Sciences—Permanence for Printed Library Materials, ANSI Z39.48-1984.

International Standard Book Number
ISBN: 978-1-68134-077-7 (hardcover)

Library of Congress Cataloging-in-Publication Data

Names: Child, Brenda J., 1959– author. | Jourdain, Gordon, translator. | Thunder, Jonathan, illustrator.
Title: Bowwow powwow : bagosenjige-niimi?idim / Brenda J. Child ; translation by Gordon Jourdain ;
    illustrations by Jonathan Thunder.
Other titles: Bagosenjige-niimi?idim
Description: Saint Paul, MN : Minnesota Historical Society Press, [2018] | Audience: Ages 3–7. | Bilingual text
    in English and Ojibwe.
Identifiers: LCCN 2017058657 | ISBN 9781681340777 (hardcover : alk. paper)
Subjects: LCSH: Powwows—Juvenile literature. | Ojibwa Indians—Juvenile literature. | Ojibwa language—
    Juvenile literature. | Ojibwa language—Texts.
Classification: LCC E98.P86 C58 2018 | DDC 497/.333—dc23
LC record available at https://lccn.loc.gov/2017058657

Bowwow POWWOW

Bagosenjige-niimi'idim

by **BRENDA J. CHILD**

Translated by **GORDON JOURDAIN**   Illustrated by **JONATHAN THUNDER**

Bowwow! Bowwow! When Windy Girl saw a lively puppy barking at a painted turtle down by the lake, she knew she had found a dog that could make her laugh. Itchy Boy was a good dog, curious and brave, but never quiet. He barked at rabbits, he barked at raccoons, and he barked at porcupines. He even barked at mosquitoes!

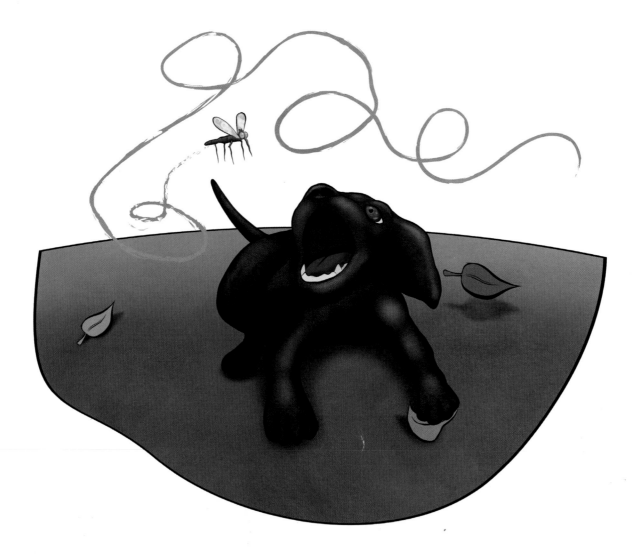

Baawaaw! Baawaw! Apii gaa-waabamaad animoonsan miginaanid miskwaadesiwan, Noodinikwens gii-kikendam gii-mikawaad animoonsan ge-ondaapid. Gii-aabezi animosh, apane wii-kikendaan gegoo miinawaa gii-soongide'e, gaawiin dash wiikaa gii-ishkwewesii. Ogii-miginaan waaboozoon, ogii-miginaan esibananjigesiwan, miinawaa ogii-miginaan gaagon. Waajigo ge ini zagimen ogii-miginaan.

Itchy Boy always barked loudest when Uncle's green pickup rolled into the yard. When they went ice fishing, he barked at the fathead minnows Windy put on her line.

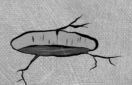

Jiichiibigwiiwizens gii-kichigizhiiwe miginaad Mishoomen bagamibizonid. Ando-wewebanaabiiwaad, ogii-miginaan ini giigoozhensan egokewid Noodinikwens.

Windy Girl and Itchy Boy knew that Uncle's pickup truck was the best place for stories. Windy especially liked to hear about the powwow. Sometimes Uncle remembered things from when he was a boy.

Noodinikwens miinawaa Jiichiibigwiiwizens gikendamoog
Mishoomen minwaajimonid ayaawaad biinjidaabaan.
Noodinikwens gii-minwedam bizindang niimi'iding. Ingoding
ako omikwendaan gii-kwiiwizensiwid Mishoome.

Uncle told Windy, "A long time ago, right before the powwow, dancers went from house to house singing. They always sang the same song, 'We are like dogs. We are like dogs.' People smiled and handed out gifts of food, maple sugar candy, and beads."

Mishoome maadaajimo, "Mewinzha, jibwaa-niimi'iding, waa-niimiwaad ako gii-
pabaa-nagamowag agwajiing endaawaad awiya. Bezhigon apane gii-izhisin nagamon,
'Gibakosenimigoo, gibakosenimigoo.' Gii-baapizhendamoog awiya miigiwewaad
wiikondiwin, ziinzibaakwadoonsan, miinawaa manidoominensag."

The story reminded Windy of Itchy Boy.

Omikwenimaan odayan Noodinikwens
noondang dibaajimowin.

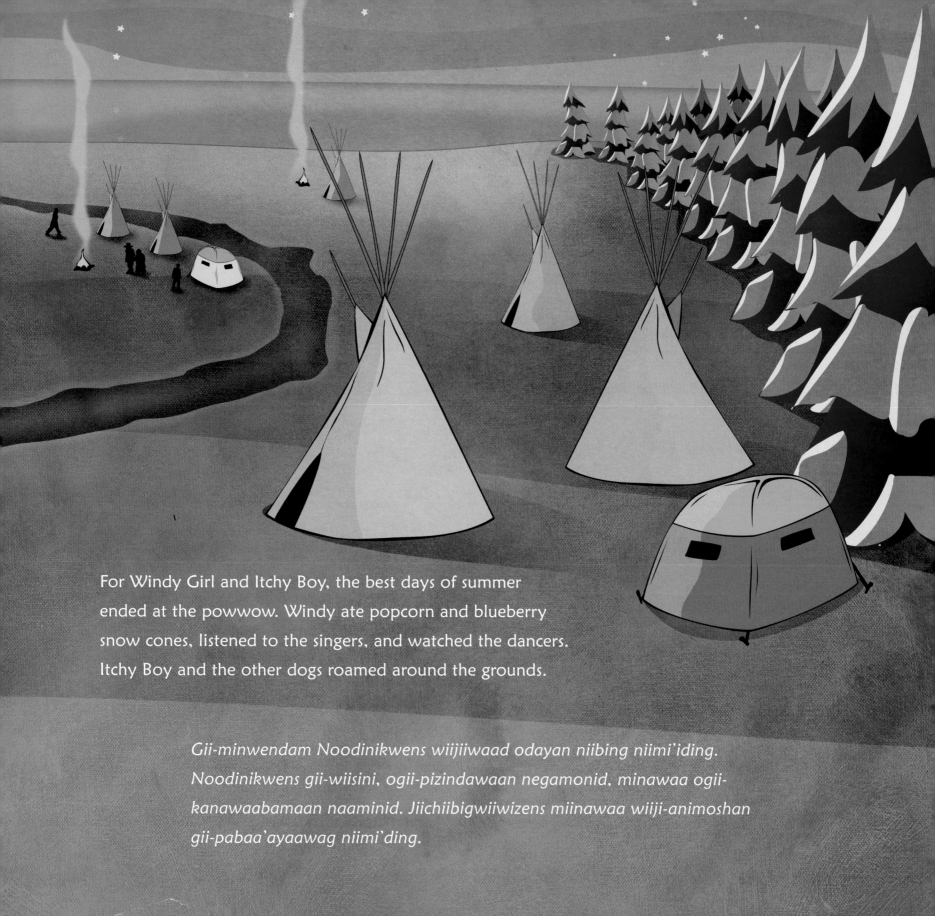

For Windy Girl and Itchy Boy, the best days of summer ended at the powwow. Windy ate popcorn and blueberry snow cones, listened to the singers, and watched the dancers. Itchy Boy and the other dogs roamed around the grounds.

Gii-minwendam Noodinikwens wiijiiwaad odayan niibing niimi'iding. Noodinikwens gii-wiisini, ogii-pizindawaan negamonid, minawaa ogii-kanawaabamaan naaminid. Jiichiibigwiiwizens miinawaa wiiji-animoshan gii-pabaa'ayaawag niimi'ding.

When a powwow is very good, and people are happy to be together singing and dancing, it sometimes lasts until late at night. Fortunately, all children and dogs love to fall asleep under the northern lights while listening to the steady heartbeat of a drum.

Kichi-minokamigad niimi'iding, baapinakamigiziwag awiya nagamowaad miinawaa niimiwaad, ingoding baamaa niibaadibik ishkwaakamigad. Abinoojiinyag miinawaa animoshag nibenkoshiwag bizindawaawaad dewe'iganan, waawaateyaa dibikad.

One night, Windy had a weird and wonderful
dream about a special powwow.

*Aabiding depikadinig, gaa-izhi-
bawaadang niimi'idiwin Noodinikwens.
Gii-maamakaadaabandam.*

Windy dreamed about the elders, who taught her to offer tobacco to express gratitude, and to dance for those unable to dance.

Noodinikwens ogii-pawaanaa' kichi-ayaa'aa', gaagii'gikino'amaagod ji-biindaakoojiged, miinawaa ji-niimitamowaad gaa-bwaanawichigenid ji-niiminid.

She dreamed about the veterans in a Grand Entry,
bearing flags and wounds from wars.

Ogii-pawaanaa' ogichidaa' biindigeshimonid, biindigatoowaad
gikiwe'onan miinawaa onjishkoozowin baniziwining.

She dreamed about a drum group, visiting from out west.

Ogii-pawaanaa' negamowaad wenjiinid ningaabii'anong.

She dreamed about the traditional dancers, dancing their style.

Ogii-pawaanaa' miigwanishimonid, ezhi-nitaa-niiminid igo.

She dreamed about the grass dancers, treading the northern earth.

Ogii-pawaanaa' mashkosiishimonid, bimikawenid giiwedino-akiikaang.

She dreamed about the jingle-dress
dancers, stepping softly to the ground.

Ogii-pawaanaa' zhiibaashka'iganishimonid,
mazinizideshimonid akiikaang.

She dreamed about the fancy
dancers, twirling bodies of color.

Ogii-pawaanaaʾ maandaawishimonid,
ezhi-nitaa-wibagizonid igo.

She dreamed about the tiny tots,
learning to move in tempo.

Ogii-pawaanaa' weshki-maajiishimonid,
ezhi-kikendaminid igo.

She even dreamed about the powwow stands
selling Indian fast food.

*Waajigo ge ogii-pawaanaa' e-daawaagenid
Anishinaabewanjigan.*

Bowwow! Bowwow! Itchy Boy's bark and the powwow announcer's voice stirred Windy awake. "Last dance tonight, folks. Everyone come out into the arena."

Baawaaw! Baawaaw! Jiichiibigwiiwizens migid miinawaa gaa-biibaagi-giigidod ogoshkomigoo' Noodinikwens. "Mii owe ishkwaaj-niimiwin noongom gaa-dibikak! Gakina awiya niminaaweshimog."

That night Windy Girl understood the powwow is always in motion, part old and part new, glittering and plain, but still wonderful, almost like a dream.

Gii-maminonendam Noodinikwens niimi'iding apane maajii'ayaa, gete'ayaa miinawaa oshki'ayaa, waake'ayaa miinawaa anisi'ayaa, memindage dash onizhshin, dibishkoo bawaajigeng.

That night Windy Girl understood the powwow is always in motion, part old and part new, glittering and plain, but still wonderful, almost like a dream.

Gii-maminonendam Noodinikwens niimi'iding apane maajii'ayaa, gete'ayaa miinawaa oshki'ayaa, waake'ayaa miinawaa anisi'ayaa, memindage dash onizhshin, dibishkoo bawaajigeng.

For Ombishkegiizhik (Frankie), Miskwaanakwadookwe (Benay), and Waaseyaanakwad (Seth). And in memory of the world's greatest service dog, Hunter. — **BJC**

To my grandchildren Bigodakamigo'inini, Waasejiwan, miinawaa Giizhigookwe. Gizhawenimin Zhooniyaa-ikwe. Apane niimiwak! — **GJ**

For my parents, Ann and Herb Thunder. Also, in honor of Waasabiikwe, Amik, Gaagigebines, and those who dedicate their lives to carrying us into the next generation. —**JT**

Author's note: *Bowwow Powwow* celebrates the history of Ojibwe song and dance, past and present. Julia Warren Spears, sister of William W. Warren, recalled the exhilarating cultural events associated with the arrival of Ojibwe clans on Madeline Island in the late summer of 1847. Spears described the form of dance that anthropologists in later years inaccurately designated as the "Begging Dance." Large parties of purposefully loud and vibrantly painted Ojibwe dancers took part in a ritual exchange of gifts. Their performances were not considered "begging" but instead displays of generosity in which friendship was enacted among extended families, clan relatives, and visitors. Songs were part of the performance and recognized the relationship between people and animals, as in the lyrics "we are like dogs, we are like dogs."